Crazy Cow

To Sally, our very own Crazy Cow

First published in hardback in Great Britain by HarperCollins Publishers Ltd in 2000
First published in paperback by Collins Picture Books in 2001

1 3 5 7 9 10 8 6 4 2
ISBN: 0-00-664718-9

A CIP catalogue record for this title is available from the British Library.

The HarperCollins website address is: www.**fire**and**water**.com

Printed and bound in Singapore by Imago

Crazy Cow

Colin and Jacqui Hawkins

An imprint of HarperCollinsPublishers

This is Crazy Cow.

Even when Crazy Cow was very young she did crazy things. Her parents were amazed. "What shall we dooo?" they mooed.

At school she did the craziest of dares, like doing a headstand on top of the school flagpole.

In gym lessons Crazy Cow was always the best. She could do somersaults, handsprings, handstands, tumble turns and back flips.

But at all the other lessons Crazy Cow was the very worst.

abcdefgh
1 × 2 = 2
2 × 2 = 2
3 × 2 = 3
1 × 2 =
1 × 2 = 2
2 × 2 = 4
3 × 2 = 6
4 × 2 = 8
5 × 2 = 10

Crazy Cow never did any of her homework – she spent all her time doing cartwheels! So when she skipped home with her school report, she landed head over heels in trouble.

"This is dreadful!" bellowed Mrs Cow. "You must stop doooing crazy things and dooo your school work."

But Crazy Cow just got crazier.

She did tightrope walking on Mrs Cow's washing line,

swung round and round on the TV aerial and then did a bungee jump off the roof!
Mr and Mrs Cow's quiet life in Meadow Lane was turned upside down by their crazy daughter.
"How will Crazy Cow ever get on in the world?" roared Mr Cow.
"What will she dooo?" mooed Mrs Cow.
But Crazy Cow never worried about anything.

Milk
Milk
Milk
THE FIELD
BULL
COW

As soon as she was old enough, Crazy Cow set off to make her fortune in the big wide world.

Mr and Mrs Cow did not see her for a long time, but she did send them lots of postcards.
"'Having a crazy time!'," read Mrs Cow. "But what's she *doooing?*" she wondered.
"Whatever it is, it'll be crazy!" snorted Mr Cow.

Milk
Mr and Mrs Cow
Meado
COW

Then, one day, the circus came to town,
and Mr and Mrs Cow went
to see the show.

In the Big Top
jugglers juggled,
the clowns
clowned,

and the fire-eater
ate fire.
It was wonderful.

Then Mr Hippo the
Ringmaster announced:
"And now, Ladies
and Gentlemen, we
present the star of the
show – the amazing,
the fantastic...

... The Great Krazo!!!"

A huge canon was trundled into the ring. The drums rolled, the fuse was lit, and... BOOM! The Great Krazo shot high into the air, and...

...turned three
somersaults, bounced
off a trampoline, did
a double back flip...

and landed perfectly in the middle of the ring. The crowd went mad and roared with delight. Everyone clapped and clapped until their hooves hurt.

Then something even crazier happened.

The Great Krazo bowed, took off her helmet and grinned at Mr and Mrs Cow.
"Wow!" gasped Mr Cow. "It's our very own Crazy Cow."
Mr and Mrs Cow were very proud. They became The Great Krazo's greatest fans and showed her photographs to all their friends.
"I'm just crazy about my Crazy Cow," mooed Mrs Cow.
"She's a star..."

"And completely CRAZY!"
bellowed Mr Cow, and they both laughed.